WARNING

This book contains sexually explicit scenes and adult language. It may be considered offensive to some readers. This book is for sale to adults ONLY.

* * * * * * * * * * * * * * * * * * *

Please store your files wisely where they cannot be accessed by underage readers.

Other Books by Darla Dunbar:

<u>The Romeo Alpha BBW Paranormal Shifter Romance Series</u>

Amanda Walker thinks that she has a normal and boring life. That is until after her 24th birthday. Everything changes when she meets the man who says he was supposed to be her husband. Denying everything the man says, she fights him every step of the way. But after he kidnaps her, Amanda discovers that there are some things about her family that her parents kept a secret all these years. Among the history of the family she learns secrets she thought only happened in story books. Can Amanda tell the difference between truth and lies or is she this mysterious woman that holds the key to a legacy?

<u>Romeo Alpha Blood Lines Romance Series</u>

Twenty-four years have passed in relative peace for Amanda and Romeo. They've raised five children into adulthood and are thoroughly enjoying their lives as the Alpha King and Queen of the werewolves. At twenty-four, Sarina is just stepping into her powers and will be ripe for mating when her birthday comes in two weeks. What no one knows is the danger that lurks just outside their tight knit community. Romeo has made peace with the other clans and has enjoyed that peace, but it will all come crashing down around him when his oldest daughter comes of age to take a mate.

The Alpha Feud BBW Paranormal Shifter Romance Series

Eliza's life consisted of reporting on boring, crowd-pleasing events, like their country livestock fair. With the arrival of two handsome brothers, the lives of Eliza and her best friend, Melissa, are shaken to the core. For Eliza, the arrival of this new man becomes a test of her relationship with her current boyfriend, who she's been happily living with for over six years. Does Hayden, a complete stranger, really wield the power to make Eliza reconsider her relationship with Andrew?

The Alpha Packed BBW Paranormal Shifter Romance Series

Darlene has led a quiet life since suffering through a terrible break-up. She wants nothing more than to spend her time in front of the TV, away from any sort of trouble. But all that goes down the drain when handsome, rugged and rough Idris comes into her life. He is a werewolf on the lookout for his missing pack leader. Darlene quickly finds herself pulled towards this mysterious man and at the same time finds herself falling deeper and deeper into the world of the supernatural.

The Daemon Paranormal Romance Chronicles

The daemon infighting can only be stopped when a strong leader emerges to calm the different factions. Juno appears to be at the heart of the conflict. Things become complicated when Phoebe and Supay try to negotiate with the siren, Juno. The love triangle among Phoebe, Supay and Apollo become tense when Juno's

meddling threatens to destroy any romance that
develops.

<u>The Mind Talker Paranormal Romance Series</u>

Ananda finds herself on the run and she's not alone.
With help from Jared, a stranger that she just met, the
two evade capture by an organization that is intent on
hunting her kind. Ananda and Jared are able to read
minds. When an unfortunate incident happened
involving a disturbed individual that resulted in the
death of his schoolmates, the secret organization
decided to take action.

Get the latest update on new releases from the
author at:

https://darladunbar.com/newsletter/

This book is Part Two of "<u>The Leather Satchel Paranormal Romance Series</u>"

Book 1 - Valtina's Redemption

Valtina is stuck in Middle World, unable to pass on to The Afterlife. In order to redeem herself from past deeds done, she must help bring romance back into the world and stop The Dark Side from destroying love in its entirety. Following orders issued by Ladaya and armed with a leather satchel filled with the appropriate tools and weapons, Valtina must bring romance back into the lives of Samantha and Joshua, thereby saving their marriage.

Book 2 - Unfaithful

Amy and Matt's relationship was never meant to be. The evil forces at work are bent on eliminating love on Earth. Couples are being mismatched in order to create chaos. It is Valtina's mission the help Amy find her soul mate and repair the damage that is being caused by the dark forces.

Book 3 - Evil Lust

Henry and Claire are meant to be together. But a succubus has taken over Henry's actions. Under her spell, Henry has succumbed to lusting after Charlotte, the human form that the succubus has assumed. If Claire were to find out, then their marriage will be ruined beyond repair. It is up to Valtina to break the succubus' spell and clear Henry's memory of any guilt that would haunt his love for Claire forever.

Book 4 - Salvaged Soul Mates

The Dark Side is winning. A Mystic has organized the evil monsters to steal every soul on Earth and leave it loveless. It is up to Valtina to do her part to save the human race. Sent by Ladaya back to Earth, Valtina's job is to unite a mismatched couple with their true soul-mates. Sebastian and Claudia were not meant to be married to each other. But a trickster was involved in encouraging the mismatch. Searching through her leather satchel, Valtina found the tools needed to do the job.

Book 5 - Fury of Lust

Valtina's missions are becoming more dangerous and will need the protection of a warrior and emere while out on duty. This time she needs to rid Rachel of a fury and free Sean of his demons. Rachel and Sean are meant to be true lovers but they have been prevented from meeting each other. Valtina must use the arsenal in her leather satchel to ensure that true love follows its course when Rachel and Sean finally meet.

Book 6 - True Lovers

Middle World has been invaded by the wraiths. While the Generals battle the monsters to protect Middle World, Valtina must continue her missions to save love on Earth. The evil forces have brain-washed Penelope and Davis into thinking that their attraction for each other is wrong. Valtina's mission is to clear the way for the couple to see that they were meant for each other and to let true love runs its fateful course.

The Leather Satchel Paranormal Romance Series

Unfaithful

Book Two

By Darla Dunbar

Copyright Revelry Publishing 2015

Table of Contents

Chapter One

EVEN THOUGH Valtina had had a great time helping Joshua and Samantha, she was having a hard time accepting the fact that her job was not yet over. After all, it was very difficult to go from thinking she was on her way to The Afterlife as a reward for finishing her job to the realization that she'd only just barely completed the first task in a list of many. She stood there, trying to come to terms with the idea that she still had a long way to go.

"So… am I really the only one who can do this job? Am I the only person you have?"

"Valtina, there are many people who can help me work with these couples, but you are by far the best at what you do. Don't think that you are the only soul at work right now. Currently, I have at least a dozen others on Earth completing their own missions. That is not your concern right now. The better you help each of these couples, the more the universe will improve and the sooner you can continue on to The Afterlife. For now, though, I need your help."

Valtina paused for a moment, wondering if she really wanted to ask her next question. She did anyway, saying, "Okay Ladaya… But just how many people are we talking about? How many more couples do I have to help along?"

"Right now, I am not sure. The Dark Side is currently working against us and they are gaining power quickly. Every day, they bring more and more people over to their side. Now, it is a matter of how many of these people we can save. We need to bring as many souls back to the light as possible, otherwise we will lose this battle forever."

Clearly, this was a very serious task. This put a great deal of pressure on Valtina and the other souls at work. "I'm going to give you some of the hardest tasks, because I know that you will be able to complete them. I will not ever give you any jobs that I don't think that you can complete. In love, you are the best person that we have."

Ladaya smiled kindly at Valtina, trying desperately to convince her. For a few minutes, Valtina mulled over her options, or at least tried to. It didn't take her long to realize that she had only one other option. However, she didn't want to be reincarnated again. After living countless lives in various bodies and time periods and situations, she was tired of all of the work and monotony. She sighed heavily, "Alright Ladaya, where do you want me to go next?"

"Next, I have a couple that is the perfect example of what will become of the world if The Dark Side wins. They feed off of misery, despair and lust. Each couple that they drag over is living in a great deal of unhappiness. Matt and Amy are the next couple that you will work with. They have been together since they were teenagers, when Matt got Amy pregnant right before their high school graduation. Although Amy never gave birth, they had already moved in together and have been living with each other ever since."

"Matt rarely gives Amy a second thought at this point. He has basically forgotten all about her, and she is completely alone. Right now, she is almost entirely dependent on Matt's income, and she can't move back in with her parents. She is trapped where she is, and she feels that she has no choice but to stay with Matt and watch as he sleeps with numerous girls on the side. You need to help get her out of there."

"Unfortunately, I do not believe that there is any hope for Matt. He has been taken too far over and he lives in lust every day. There is very little that can be done for him at this point, although we may be able to help him further down the road. For now though, we will have to focus on getting Amy to a better place… I have been keeping an eye on the situation for some time now, trying to determine what the best option would be for her. I want you to bring her to Kyle, a man who lives in the same apartment building. Do what you can for her. Here is your leather satchel. I've added a few items for your quest. Take care."

Ladaya was much more abrupt in this encounter, trying to get rid of Valtina faster so that she didn't have any time to protest or ask questions. The less time she had to think over the mission, the better. So, as soon as she stopped speaking, Ladaya transported Valtina to Amy and Matt's apartment building.

Chapter Two

Valtina traveled through space and time, watching the fog and mist disperse as she reached her destination. In the matter of only a few seconds, she had left Middle World and returned to Earth yet again. This time, she appeared in a dark alley in a neighborhood that must have been a lower class residential area. The worn brick of the apartment building next to her didn't seem trustworthy, and Valtina walked out from the alley toward the main road.

As she turned the corner, she saw a young man getting out of his car and jogging around the front of it. As he turned, he lost his balance and started to fall. After barely catching himself, he started laughing along with the girl in the passenger seat. They were both smiling as he opened the door for her and reached his hand out as an offering. She took it saying, "Thanks for the ride, Matt."

For a moment, Valtina was confused. She had automatically assumed that this man and woman were Matt and Amy, though it appeared she was only half correct. Seeing movement out of the corner of her eye, she saw a woman standing in an upstairs window, watching the scene taking place below. The sadness on her face was contagious and Valtina instantly sympathized with her. She left the window, turning away from her boyfriend. This was probably a smart choice because Matt leaned in and kissed the young woman as he pulled her from his car.

"Anytime, baby doll. You sure you don't want me to drive you the other block back to your apartment? Maybe I could stay for a while."

"Matt, I'm sure that your girlfriend is waiting for you already. You don't need to make me feel even guiltier!"

"She doesn't mind. It's not like we have any plans for tonight anyway."

"No Matt, thanks for the offer but I'll be fine walking… it's just a little bit further anyway." She turned and waved over her shoulder, walking away from him. She swayed her hips when she walked and he couldn't take his eyes off her ass.

"Hate to see you go, but love to watch you leave!" he called after her. Then he went inside, up the stairs to his apartment. Valtina followed close behind, despite her disgust at being so near him.

When they entered the apartment, it was easy to see that they didn't have a lot of money. It seemed most of this apartment was filled with cheap DIY furniture and cheap decorations. Although it was obvious that there wasn't a large budget for this home, it was also easy to see that a great deal of attention and consideration went into every aspect of the place. Valtina could feel Amy's energy coming from every direction. She was waiting on a bar stool at the kitchen counter as Valtina and Matt entered.

"Hey babe. How was work?"

"It was fine. Is dinner ready?" He walked over without glancing at her, picked up the plate of food that was set out for him, and took it to a recliner. He sat down, flipped on the TV, and took a bite of the food. He was served chicken and rice, and she automatically walked over to take out a cold beer from the refrigerator.

"Chicken's cold," he said gruffly.

"Sorry, I had it ready but you're a little later coming home than you usually are."

"Well, you can heat it up again."

She put the beer down on the counter, bowed her head, and took the plate. As she was doing this, Valtina removed a clear, colorless potion from the leather satchel and poured a few drops in the beer. After placing the plate in the microwave oven, Amy handed Matt the beer and returned to the kitchen. In a few minutes, Amy returned to Matt to serve the reheated chicken. She walked in a depressed manner, as though she was completely terrified of the man that she lived with. As she handed him the plate of food, she watched expectantly, waiting to see if he enjoyed it more this time around.

He took a bite, swallowed, and nodded his satisfaction. She did not receive a thank you or any other form of acknowledgement, but she was happy with that.

"Do you mind if I go for a walk?" It was as though she was asking permission to leave the apartment.

"Go ahead, but I want you back in ten minutes. I'll be done eating by then and you can do the dishes before I have to take a shower."

She nodded again and went to grab a jacket. Valtina noticed several bruises around her arms, as though she had been roughly grabbed several times. While Valtina encouraged a little roughness in the bedroom, there was nothing good about being in an abusive relationship. She was immediately filled with rage as she followed Amy out the door.

Valtina realized that she had to find this 'Kyle' quickly. Otherwise, there will be major problems for Amy. Although she was unsure of where to start, she knew that she was not going to stand around in an apartment with Matt while he drank beer and watched wrestling on television.

As she watched Amy, Valtina was surprised when Amy turned to her right as she left her apartment, rather than going left toward the stairs that was to take them down and out. Amy, instead, headed upwards a few flights of stairs. Before following, Valtina removed a key from her leather satchel and locked the apartment door behind her. She caught up to Amy as she reached the top level. Amy didn't stop there, however, and continued up a little bit more, pushing open the door to the roof. This didn't appear like something new to

Amy, and Valtina was immediately sure that this was something she frequently did to get away from Matt when he was around. Now that she was away from him and had a little more privacy, Amy looked like a completely different person. She was quite beautiful and she looked slightly more relaxed than she had been in her boyfriend's presence.

Slowly, gracefully, she walked over toward to the edge of the building and sat down in a chair that overlooked the rest of the neighborhood, with the city skyline off a little way in the distance. Even though this was a very poor area, there was something beautiful about this view. She watched the sun setting behind the city while Valtina studied her. Valtina had remnants of a plan percolating in her head. Neither of them noticed when the roof door pushed open a second time and a man stepped through.

"How often do you come up here? It seems you're always here when I come."

Amy jumped in shock, turned to see who it was and immediately smiled, relaxing a little. "Sometimes I feel like you're stalking me, given how often we run into each other."

Valtina waited, trying to figure out who the man was. Amy motioned to the chair next to her while the man lit a cigarette and shook his head. He didn't sit next to her but instead walked a little closer, off to the side. "I'd sit with you, but secondhand smoke is bad for you."

She shrugged, "It's not any better firsthand, is it?"

He shrugged in response. Valtina was surprised by his consideration as he stood only upwind of her, so that none of the smoke blew back against her. "So, what are you up here for this time? Fresh air again?"

"Sure, fresh air is good."

"You know, living in the apartment over you, I can hear the way he talks to you Amy. I don't know why you bother staying with him. He's no good for you, or any of the whores he always has with him. How do you stand it?"

Her expression immediately darkened. Clearly, she was like most people and didn't like people digging into her business. "I don't know how I stand you. I should move, or take out a restraining order."

She stood up abruptly and walked towards the door. Even though she appeared angry, the glance back over her shoulder as she left just showed that she was afraid. Probably afraid of what Matt would do if anything happened, of the unknown, of change. That's what happens when a girl is trapped somewhere that she doesn't want to be. Even though she wanted out more than anything, the idea of landing herself in a worse situation than where she started off is often enough to keep her from doing anything at all.

Valtina could sense the attraction between the man and Amy, even if neither of them did at that moment. Amy paused just inside the door to the building, a couple steps down from the roof, still thinking about the man. It was through her thoughts that Valtina discovered the man was Kyle. He was the man that

Ladaya wanted her to be with. While Amy considered whether or not she should go back to her apartment, Valtina was busy considering different options for getting Amy and Kyle together.

Amy sighed, checked her watch and decided that she didn't have enough time to go for an actual walk around the block. And she didn't want to be lingering in the hallway when Kyle finished his cigarette on the roof. So she shuffled reluctantly back down the stairs to her apartment. She sighed again before attempting to open the door. As she turned the knob, she found that the door to the apartment was locked. Valtina could sense the panic in her mind as she searched through her pockets for her keys and realized they weren't there. At the same time, she knew that this happened frequently to her. Matt was inside the apartment, audibly snoring and Amy was locked out.

While Amy banged on the door and called her boyfriend's name, Valtina took a moment to reflect on her plan. On the rooftop, Kyle extinguished his cigarette and made his way back inside. Although Matt would probably have woken up eventually, the sexual spirit made certain that the sleeping potion would keep him in a deep sleep. This way, as Kyle came down the stairs to his apartment, he would hear her banging and calling for her boyfriend to let her in.

With just a little persuading, Kyle stepped in to play the hero.

"Hey… Are you alright?"

"I'm fine… Just…" Quickly, Valtina had to work to make sure that Amy relaxed enough to let Kyle in. She was a bit more difficult to work with, after being in this situation so long.

"He locked you out?"

"He probably didn't do it on purpose. Just locked the door and assumed I had the keys, that's all. There's no real problem with that, is there?"

"If that's all, then why isn't he letting you back in?"

Amy paused for a moment until, finally, her thoughts were gently broken through and pushed in the right direction. "He's not refusing to let me back in. He's probably just passed out drunk in the chair, that's all." She frowned slightly, her forehead creasing in worry and frustration.

"Do you have your cell phone?"

"Yeah, I have it. Why?"

"Why don't you just come upstairs to my apartment and wait it out? Text him, leave him a voicemail, whatever. I'm sure he'll get back to you when he wakes up. I don't really like the thought of you waiting out in the hallway. He could be out for the night."

Amy and Valtina both noticed the hint of hopefulness in his worried tone. While Valtina took that as a good sign for the direction things would lead, it was still something that led Amy to doubt him a little. Although this might have been a more difficult task for Valtina, she was much more excited about this one because of how much laid on her shoulders. She put an extra amount of effort into convincing Amy that it would be a good idea to spend some time with Kyle.

She had to think about it for a few minutes before deciding to go along with it, "Alright, that's fine. Thank you for letting me wait with you. I appreciate it."

"No problem," he said flashing a winning smile. She couldn't help but notice how attractive he was. It was immediately clear that he had a rough appearance, but upon further inspection he was also quite handsome. He had an angular face with sharp, chiseled features which were softened slightly by the way his hair fell around his face. Although he probably didn't spend much time on his appearance, his jeans and flannel shirt fit him nicely. There was some rough stubble around his chin where he hadn't shaved, and although he may not be the most clean-cut man Amy had ever seen, he had a warm smile and dark brown eyes. Plus, he was much better looking than Matt.

She walked up the stairs to his landing, trying not to think about the fact that she just discovered how appealing she found this man. In all truth, Matt would probably be quite angry with her just for having those thoughts, let alone going into his apartment with him.

Kyle opened the door and let Amy enter first. Valtina fell close behind, wanting to see everything at the same time Amy did to better gauge her reaction. His apartment was mostly clean, although there were a few dishes in the sink and some empty cans of soda on the coffee table. It was still much more organized and well-furnished than either Amy or Valtina had expected it to be. As Kyle closed the door behind them, he laughed.

"I know it's not much to look at, sorry for that. You can have a seat anywhere you like… this might be a long night."

She walked in a little bit, choosing to take a seat on the couch. The only other options for seating were a few bar stools along the kitchen counter. He turned and hung his keys on a hook by the door then headed into the kitchen area and got himself a glass of water. "Is there anything that I can get for you? Did you eat dinner before you got locked out?"

"I don't usually eat dinner… But I'm fine, thank you. You do have a nice apartment."

"Thanks. So, what would you like to do in the meantime?"

With the help of her new spirit follower, a thought poped into her head that she never would have had before. For a split second, she imagined the feeling of his lips on her neck. Valtina tried to project similar images into Kyle's mind as well, but it was difficult to be sure if it worked or not. He kept a straight face while he waited for an answer.

"Oh, I'd be fine with just about anything. It's your apartment… you can do what you want. Do you have any plans for tonight? I would hate to interrupt."

"No," he laughed. "I had just been planning on doing the dishes, microwaving some dinner, and watching TV till it got late enough for bed."

She cringed slightly, "You were going to microwave dinner?"

"Yeah, just one of those frozen things you pop in for a few minutes. They're not that bad, really."

"They are that bad. You need someone who can cook." As she said it, she couldn't help but blush, thinking that it might be fun to cook for someone who would appreciate it.

He took advantage of this moment, "You know, if you feel so strongly about this, then maybe you could show me what a home-cooked meal actually tastes like? I can't remember the last time I actually had food that didn't have to be defrosted first."

"Do you have anything to cook with?"

"I've got some food. I buy it every now and then, in case I'm inspired to be a chef for the night. You can go through all my stuff in the kitchen."

Chapter Three

He led the way, pulling open cupboards and indicating certain foods that might be useful. Eventually, Amy pulled out a bag of rice, some chicken that was in the freezer, and some seasonings. She got to work, and while she defrosted the chicken, Kyle stood close by.

His presence distracted her while she cooked, but he was so drawn in by her that he couldn't help it. His eyes never left her while she worked, and he couldn't really understand why he felt the need to be so close to her, but he didn't fight it. Instead, he tried to make it a little more normal by offering his assistance. "What can I do to help?"

Immediately, she put him to work watching the rice, because it was clear that he would be little help elsewhere. While she worked and he stood there, pretending to be useful, they talked. "So, if it's not too personal for me to ask, why do you stay with Matthew?"

She frowned slightly, concentrating on cutting the chicken. "It's not like I have much choice."

"Why not?"

"Well, because… we've been together for a long time. I clearly haven't had many opportunities. I don't work, I can't afford a place of my own, and it's not like I have that many options for places to stay."

"But he's awful to you."

"He didn't use to be, and he isn't always."

"He should never be." Kyle stood up with brows furrowed and his hands in his pockets, trying to think of ways to say things in a more appropriate manner. The harder he tried, the more he struggled. Valtina, on the other hand, worked to lead this conversation to more inappropriate areas.

She sighed, "Still, where would I go? It's not like there're people dying to let me live with them."

"You could stay with me," he blurted out, unable to help himself. Amy smiled and laughed.

"Yeah, that's totally normal. I know we've known each other for a while, but it's not exactly as if we really know each other."

"Is that really all that important? I know that you need somewhere to stay and you don't deserve that damn awful boyfriend that you're trapped with now. You don't have to stay forever, just long enough to get yourself on your own two feet and away from that lowlife."

"I'll think about it. Thanks for the offer… why do you want to help me anyway?"

"Maybe living over someone for six months and hearing the way their man yells at them makes me feel like it's my responsibility. Plus, you're hot."

As he said it, both of their eyes widened. He hadn't meant to say it and she certainly hadn't been expecting it. She turned to face him, "Sorry, I'm not sure that I heard that right. What did you just say?" Despite how much he tried not to repeat himself, Valtina stepped in and fought him to say it. When she eventually succeeded, the words traveled from his mouth in a jumbled cluster at first.

Kyle leaned down, looking in her bright green eyes. "You really are very attractive, you know. I don't understand how a man could have a woman like you and treat her the way that he does. It's wrong. One day, he'll get what he deserves… I just hope that you get what you deserve sooner, and I hope that it makes you happy."

Amy frowned slightly. She didn't mean to, but she had been imagining the taste of his lips ever since she first saw him tonight, and her mind wasn't any clearer now. "Sorry, I'm not entirely sure what you're saying…"

Her heart fluttered in her chest… she was filled with nervousness and excitement, and maybe even a hint of longing as they stared into each other's eyes. For a moment they were both quiet while Kyle tried to work up the nerve to say or do something else. Finally, he leaned in just a little bit closer and whispered, "You know I would like to make you happy."

"What do you mean?" Her face flushed with excitement.

"I mean that you deserve someone who will treat you right and make you happy, and I think that I could be the one to do that." Without thinking (Valtina wouldn't let him think about it), he reached out and pulled her closer in his excitement, kissing her roughly, passionately. Amy didn't resist the kiss and after a few moments she started kissing him back. By the time they came up for air, they were both panting for breath and flushed with excitement.

"Right now, all that I know is that I need this. I need you. I don't want to think about the consequences that I might have to face, and I want to completely forget about Matt right now, if you're willing to help erase my thoughts for a little bit longer…" Towards the end, she faltered a little, thinking that he might not want to keep going. She didn't have to worry for long, however.

Before she could think about saying anything else, he was pulling her to him, picking her up off the ground, and carrying her without letting their lips part. She had never realized how strong he was, although she supposed she should have expected it, considering how much time he spent working out in the sun. He was able to lift her without a problem, wrap her legs around him, and completely transport her body to the couch, while he transported her mind to a whole different universe using his lips.

Amy was breathless and excited, growing hot with every touch and movement. Matt was desperate, having waited for this moment for a long time. Even if neither of them knew it yet, Valtina knew just how perfect they were for each other and they would soon be falling in love. Without letting herself think, Amy reached up from underneath Matt and slipped her hands under his shirt, feeling his warm chest, enjoying his heartbeat through his skin.

"May I?" he asked breathlessly, seeking permission to touch her in more personal areas.

"Please do…" she moaned, tugging at the hem of his shirt, lifting it over his head, pulling it off before he started on hers.

Soon, they were both panting and clutching at each other, Matt lying on top of her half-naked body on the couch. Before she left her apartment, she hadn't bothered to put on a bra, so she was completely exposed. Kissing her neck, Matt started massaging her breasts, squeezing and playing with them, taking extra care to stimulate her nipples. She gasped in pleasure as she reached around, grabbing his ass. She blushed as she did this, then slipped her hands under the belt of his pants and teased him.

He enjoyed her touch while she enjoyed his lips at her collar bone. Soon, her hands had returned to his front, still inside his pants. Already, he was completely hard from the excitement. It was clear that he was enjoying this. As she grasped his hardening length, he panted breathlessly and rolled over onto his back. Instinctively, Amy climbed on top of him, though not before she stripped him down completely naked. She paused for a moment, admiring the look of his bare skin, the soft curls of hair at his stomach, and his well-defined muscles before she mounted him. She couldn't help but attack him with kisses, grinding herself against his cock, her clothes barely separating their skin.

His hands teased her nipples while they kiss, making them grow even harder and more sensitive. She started moving lower, sucking on his neck, reaching lower again to tease his cock. She moved her hands up and down, stimulating him, feeling him grow even larger while she did this. Slowly, she reached to caress his balls while she kissed down his chest. He lay back, enjoying every touch.

The further down she moved, the more excited Amy became. She could feel her panties growing moist. Although Matt was not the only man she had ever been with, it had been several years since she had been with anyone else. The idea of someone new excited her even further. She stood up, feeling the desperate need to be naked now. Following her movements, Kyle sat up on the couch and helped undress her. He leaned toward Amy, kissing her abs and pulling at her waistband, slowly removing her clothes. Although they moved passionately, touching and kissing the whole time, they moved slowly, taking their time and moving rhythmically, savoring the entire experience.

Never in her life had Amy been so excited. Every touch was driving her insane, sending goose bumps down her spine as she shook with the pleasure. Kyle admired her naked body, placing delicate and loving kisses over her entire body.

He held her in his arms, turning her on her back, spreading her legs and climbing between them, still kissing her neck. "Are you okay with doing this?"

She couldn't help but remember that her boyfriend was right below them, probably directly underneath them. Amy smiled, "I don't think I've ever been so okay with something in my life. Now fuck me."

The words sent chills down both of their spines and they were instantly together, connected, combined, and there was no way that they could be closer. He thrust into her, feeling the way her tightness squeezed him. He was not exactly large, but he was bigger than Matt and she gasped in slight pain before she was overcome with complete pleasure. For a moment, he paused over her, making sure she was alright and enjoying the way she filled around him. Her hands explored his body while he started moving against her, pulling back and thrusting deep into her. Each movement made them breathe a little harder against each other. Amy knotted her hands in his hair, feeling her vaginal muscles tense around his hard cock, buried deep inside of her. She was struggling to see straight through the pleasure and the oncoming orgasm.

She moaned, trying not to scream out and wake Matt downstairs. Nevertheless, she whispered into Kyle's ear, "I'm going to come!"

With these words, he reacted and started pounding her harder, going deeper inside of her with each thrust. "I want to feel you explode with my cock inside you." She moaned in complete ecstasy, her nails cutting into his back as she climaxed. He kept thrusting into her, his hands tangled in her hair, pulling her head up, making her look him in the eye as she reached orgasm. She moaned, trying to see straight… she breathed his name while she trembled, waves of pleasure washing through her entire body, extending even into the tips of her fingers and her toes.

Kyle let her relax for a moment, collapsing on top of her, wiping a bead of sweat off her forehead. "I never knew it was possible, but you look even more beautiful now." He kept kissing her while he waited for Amy's breathing to return to normal. It took a while of waiting before the orgasm was over… never before had she experienced something so powerful. The excitement of being with someone new and doing something so wrong, with a man who was so sexy, helped to push her even further over the edge. Even after she had managed to calm her breathing, she still shook slightly underneath Kyle.

"That was... amazing."

"Well, we're not done just yet, are we?"

She looked up at him, quizzically. "You didn't cum yet?"

"I wanted to, but I wasn't wearing a condom... I was wondering, have you ever tried... anal?"

She blushed profusely, trying to imagine something like that, especially with him. "No, I haven't ever tried."

"Well, looks like you'll get the chance to now." He started getting up, surprising her as he went to the bedroom. He returned a moment later, carrying a bottle of lubricant.

Amy was immediately more nervous but she decided that it was in her best interest to keep calm and go with it. She had always wondered what it would be like, but Matt never suggested it and she never brought up the issue. Besides, she didn't think that Kyle would ever hurt her and they've been having such an incredible time. Plus, even she had to admit that there was a part of her that wanted to know what it felt like to have a man inside her ass. Even though she had never even used fingers on herself there, she fantasized about it. She was growing wetter with excitement now, imagining how it would feel if Kyle stretched her most forbidden hole and filled her with his seed.

"What do you need me to do?" she blushed, embarrassed and excited, hardly able to look at him as she imagined what was about to happen to her.

"Babe, right now all I need you to do is lie down on your stomach and relax."

Amy did as she was told and lay flat on the couch, with her ass completely exposed to him. Her flush spread across her entire body, tinting even her lower cheeks a lovely pink that made Kyle even harder. He grabbed her gently, though passionately, by the ankles and spun her around slightly, so that her thighs hung over the edge of the couch and he spread her legs apart, taking his spot close to her, kneeling on the ground.

He took care to lube his fingers, squirting a little onto the tips of his index and middle fingers. Gently, he separated her ass cheeks, enjoying the clean, puckered hole revealed. Slowly, he massaged the lubricant there, moistening her and easing her to the entrance of his fingertips.

"Tell me if it hurts… It might hurt a little at first, but I really want you to enjoy this."

As he spoke the words, Kyle gently pushed his finger past her anus, entering her darkest opening, where no one else had ever explored. A shiver of excitement flooded her. It didn't hurt, although she felt definite pressure… to her, one single finger felt much larger and she wondered whether or not she would be able to fully take his penis into her later on.

After a moment of letting her adjust to this new form of penetration, he pushed further, deeper, until his entire middle finger was inside her. In just a few moments, she had grown accustomed to this foreign invasion and she was already starting to enjoy it as he slowly moved his finger in and out of her, thrusting gently but building force and speed with each movement deeper into her.

She couldn't help but cry out a few times in slight pain or surprise at having something inside her ass, especially as he inserted a second finger into her and started moving it roughly in and out, fucking her anus. To help her enjoy it more, Kyle reached with his other hand and rubbed her clit hard and fast, sending pleasure through her core. She clutched a pillow and buried her face in it, trying to prevent herself from screaming out with both pain and pleasure. Although she was enjoying the anal stimulation and she was shaking from the pleasure that it caused her, she was still worried about how badly it would hurt to have something as large as his cock inside her.

"How does it feel Amy?"

"It's really good… I'm so tight though. Do you really think I'm going to be able to handle your dick? I'm happy to try if you think I can, but I don't know how you will be able to fit…"

Knowing that she was willing to give it a try, he responded by rubbing a third finger at her entrance. Before even attempting to push it inside of her and stretch her to her limits, he opened the bottle of lube and squirted another generous glob onto her anus, rubbing it in and watching the goose bumps spread across her entire body.

"Please, be gentle..." she begged, not meaning to speak the words out loud. Her voice was filled with concern and worry, but there was also still an audible amount of excitement and need there. Kyle ignored her plea, choosing not to answer her… instead he spread her ass cheeks roughly and continued applying the thick goo across her tight hole. Quickly, he eased his third finger inside of her, stretching her.

Kyle grew harder at Amy's sudden intake of breath, enjoying the delicious way that her puckered hole stretched to accommodate three digits. Although he was enjoying her squirming, he was gentle enough to let her get used to the invasion before he started moving in and out of her. The entire time while he waited, he teased her clit gently, enjoying the way that her juices started to flow more and more with each passing moment. Without warning her, he slowly started moving his fingers back and forth inside her tight asshole. She bit down on her hand… her eyes started to water with the enjoyable sensations and the pain that he was delivering to her private areas. Once she got used to the feeling of so many of his fingers buried deep inside her, she couldn't help but moan in pleasure, fully enjoying how good it felt, despite the soreness in her ass. Starting to finger-fuck her harder, he moved his hand away from her clit and spanked her hard instead.

She let out a yelp, too excited to feel any real pain, and he gave several more harsh slaps on her ass. The excitement built in both of them… Kyle grew larger and harder than ever while Amy's pussy flooded with moisture.

"Babe, I can't wait any more. I think you're ready, and I know that you can handle my cock buried deep inside you... just relax."

Slowly he withdrew his fingers and stood, positioning himself behind her, rubbing her natural juices from her pussy into her anus and onto his cock. Rubbing the head of his erect penis against her tight opening, he started slowly entering her. It took a few moments to work her up to it, but it didn't take long before he was able to push himself in, the first inch of his length popping in fairly easily. As he entered, she let out a soft squeal, clutching the pillow tighter and clenching her fist, unable to help it. Kyle closed his eyes in pleasure, allowing her to get used to his thick dick inside her once more. He had to be patient now if he had any hope of her letting him continue. While he tried to move deeper, sliding inch by inch into her virgin hole, stretching her even more than she ever imagined she could be, he reached up to stroke her clit, helping her relax and making her wetter than ever.

"Please," she begged. "Please, just fuck me now, I need it. I need you."

Until now however, she hadn't realized that he wasn't entirely inside her. In a rush of passion and excitement, Kyle pushed himself all the way inside her, each and every inch of his length buried deep within her muscular inner walls. She let out a sharp cry of pain but this time he didn't stop and wait… he didn't have any more patience left in him now, as he started pounding away at her tight anus. She clenched her teeth, trying to keep from being too loud as her eyes started to water and tears streamed down her face. As he humped her, going deeper and harder with each ruthless thrust, she was sure that she was going to burst from being stretched so far. Even though he felt very large when he was filling her pussy, she had not expected him to feel so much larger inside her asshole.

After a few minutes of him thrusting deep into her, making her eyes water, the pain slowly morphed into pleasure, sending more incredible sensations through her entire body. It made her feel things that she had never experienced before and she couldn't believe how good it felt. Meanwhile, he was so close to climaxing that he was unable to think… only to feel. Both Kyle and Amy tried not to cum, wanting the feelings to last as long as possible but soon neither of them was able to resist the pleasure coursing through them.

Soon, Kyle was pumping his seed deep inside her, filling her in ways she enjoyed more than she would have imagined. As he shook, collapsing on top of her, Amy was overcome with her own orgasm. Her entire body was flooded with pleasure and the warmth and weight of Kyle's body pressing down on her only intensified this. Together, the two of them remained on the couch, sweating and shaking, unable to move or think clearly. Then Amy surrendered herself to the quaking magnitude of the orgasm, and she wasn't sure how long she had been lying there underneath Kyle before either of them spoke.

"You're not going back."

She started to respond but stopped, trying to understand what he was saying. "What?"

"I don't want you going back to Matt."

"Where do you want me to go then?"

"Stay here. I can get your stuff while he's at work tomorrow, and you'll never have to talk to him again. I don't care if you and I don't last… you don't have to be with me just because I let you stay here. I just want to know that you're safe. I can't stand the idea of you going back."

After a moment of silence, Kyle asked, "Well…
what do you think?"

"… You're squishing me…"

He laughed and climbed off of her, helping her sit
up on the couch. "Well?"

"Well…" She blushed, feeling much shyer now
than she had just a few minutes earlier. "Are you sure? I
mean, I don't want to impose…"

Adjusting their position on the couch, Kyle
carefully enclosed her in his arms, pulling her close and
stroking her hair gently. "I might not be the greatest
man on earth, but I know a good woman when I see
one, and I want you to be safe. You don't have to stay
with me, but I'm not letting you go back to him, one
way or another. And Amy, I would be very happy if
you would come and live with me."

She looked at him, nodding her head, happy that she
might have found peace. After their orgasms, however,
they both fell asleep quickly, in each other's arms on
the couch.

Over the next day, Valtina kept close watch, not
wanting to leave until things had settled down.
Watching with particular attention to Matt, she stood
inside the doorway, as he moved throughout his
apartment, looking for any remaining traces of Amy.

He couldn't find anything that she could have
forgotten, and not having any dinner waiting for him

after a long day of work, he was especially disappointed. Matt eventually came to the realization that Amy wasn't there anymore. He frantically searched for anything, clutching at the hope that she might be there somewhere, but in his rage he did nothing but trash his apartment. Still observing, Valtina's attention was caught by a slight movement behind Matt.

For a moment, she watched, trying to determine what it was. After she stared for a few moments, she could make out a form that slowly appeared just behind him. The figure standing there carried a sense of familiarity, and Valtina immediately thought of her own position, following Amy and ensuring that she found what she needed in order to fall in love. As she watched this figure, however, she realized that there was something a little different now. He wasn't watching in a way that seemed to 'guide' Matt on the right path… in fact, Valtina couldn't figure out exactly what he was doing.

The ghostly man looked over at Valtina and smirked. He controlled Matt like a puppet, giving him strict instructions rather than gently guiding him as Valtina had done with Amy. Matt had little willpower left to be his own person. He was completely powerless against his controller and Valtina's heart sank… her job just got much harder. The Dark Side had agents at work as well.

-*To be continued in Book 3*-

If you enjoyed this title, I would appreciate your leaving a review of the book. Good reviews encourage an author to write as well as help books to sell. Good reviews can be just a few short sentences describing what you liked about the book without having a spoiler. If you could spend 30 seconds writing a review, I would appreciate it: you can review this title right now at your favorite retailer.

Here is a preview of the **next story** you may enjoy:

Evil Lust - The Leather Satchel Paranormal Romance Series, Book 3

VALTINA WAITED patiently for Ladaya to return with her next assignment. She didn't know how much time had passed since she last saw her mentor. Time ran differently in Middle World, much more slowly than on Earth or in The Afterlife. Valtina had stopped trying to keep up with it several lifetimes ago, but Ladaya's absence seemed long, even by Middle World standards.

As she waited, Valtina wondered where Ladaya would send her next. She was determined to earn her way into The Afterlife, and she was full of confidence that she would be successful. Her recent mission had been challenging but rewarding… Amy and Kyle were meant to be together. Matt was a lost cause and Valtina was able to finesse the situation for the best outcome. In just two days, she was able to create a long-lasting relationship that should have happened a lot sooner. Valtina was certain she could handle any assignment Ladaya gave her.

The last assignment was actually enjoyable. In fact, Valtina would probably have accepted the mission even if Ladaya hadn't offered The Afterlife as a reward. In each of her lives, Valtina had been a passionate, sexual person. She'd never enjoyed sex just for the sake of sex. In each life she'd found her soul-mate, the one person whose spirit understood hers. And in each life, she and her soul-mate had enjoyed passionate, adventurous sex.

"I guess I am uniquely qualified for this job," Valtina thought out loud.

"You certainly are," said a familiar voice behind her. Valtina turned and found Ladaya approaching. She looked tired… and a little worried.

"Are you alright?" Valtina asked.

"It's been a long three days." Ladaya sighed. "We're losing ground. We've tapped every resource we have, but evil is still winning. Their numbers are multiplying as ours dwindle. There's still hope, of course, I just never thought it would get this far." Ladaya smiled sadly.

"What can I do, Ladaya?" Valtina asked determinedly.

"We're fighting many dark forces," Ladaya explained, "forces that for centuries were happy to fight amongst themselves. Humans have always been affected by them, but never to such a large scale. But a few decades ago, these forces decided to unite under a common goal. Since then, their sole focus has been to end existence as we know it. And, as you know, the only way to do that is to rid the world of love. If the last drop of love dies, every living organism will follow… the barren earth will be left to every foul creature that's ever been created. I'm sorry if this sounds repetitive, Valtina, but you MUST understand the importance of your missions."

"I understand, Ladaya. Just tell me where to go next."

"This case is much different than your last mission," Ladaya began. "Claire and Henry are married, and they're meant to be. But there are forces working against them… powerful forces. In fact, Valtina, I'm about to put you up against, essentially, your evil twin."

"My evil twin? I'm afraid I'm going to need you to explain that," Valtina said, taken aback.

"Think Valtina. Your strength, your love, your goodness, they're all rooted in your sexuality. What's the evil counterpart to that?"

Valtina thought for a moment, and then gasped. "You can't be serious," she said firmly. "They don't exist. Not anymore."

"That's what we thought, but we were wrong. I think they've been waiting… the other creatures have set everything up just right, and now they've come out of hiding and they're moving in for the final play."

"So… you're sending me after…"

"Yes. A succubus," Ladaya interrupted. "I'm not sure of her true name, but Henry knows her as Charlotte. It's important that we move quickly. Henry has only been under her spell for a few days. Claire and Henry have a nine-month-old baby, so Claire is distracted and hasn't noticed any change in her husband. If we can keep her from finding out, we can save their marriage. We could wipe her memory, but we can't erase the scars left by that deep of a betrayal. If she learns of Henry's infidelity, their love will die."

"We won't let evil win Ladaya, I'll do my best work." Valtina took her friend by the hand and met her eyes. "My absolute best work. I promise."

"You must Valtina." She sighed, squeezing her hand. "Once you've broken the spell Charlotte has on Henry, wipe his memory of her. He isn't cheating on purpose… she has total control. This isn't something he should suffer for."

"But how do I break the spell?" Valtina asked.

"Follow your instincts," Ladaya smiled. "This is one area in which they've always served you well. Now, you'd probably be able to spot the succubus anyway, but your new powers will allow you to see her true form. You'll see the true form of other creatures as well. Do NOT react when you see them. Some monsters can see spirits, so you don't want to draw attention to yourself. If you're ever in true danger I'll sense it, and I'll send help immediately."

Valtina wasn't scared. As a matter of fact, this was the most exhilarated she'd felt since she entered Middle World. Once again, she had a purpose, a reason for being. "What do you want me to do with the succubus after I've broken her spell?" she asked fiercely.

"Nothing," Ladaya responded firmly. "You are to focus on your mission, and your mission alone. We have others in our ranks who are equipped to fight monsters. But the connection between her and Henry must be broken first, or anything we do to her will happen to him too."

"I'll do it as quickly as possible," Valtina promised. "I'll see you soon." She smiled at Ladaya as the fog surrounded her, transporting her to Henry and Claire's bedroom.

If you enjoyed this sample then look for **Evil Lust - The Leather Satchel Paranormal Romance Series, Book 3.**

Here is a preview of **another story** you may enjoy:

The Shifter - The Daemon Paranormal Romance Chronicles, Book 2

WALKING OUT of the hotel room, Phoebe jumped back in surprise. Her dog, Ace, ran up to her. "Ace! What are you doing here?" She leaned down to pet him. "Come inside with me and we will get you something to eat."

Bringing him inside with her, she glanced over at Apollo. She met his questioning eyes with a shrug. "I have no clue how he got here. It seems impossible, but here he is."

Apollo shrugged. "Weirder things have happened. I guess we can just bring him along with us. Having him could help." Standing up, he grabbed the bag of weapons and restraints. Together, they left the room and got in the car.

Parking near the jade shop, the pair sipped coffee as they waited for Qilin to close the shop. They inched the car along behind her as she went to a park. The sunlight was quickly fading away and few people were in the park. Quickly, they got out of the car and followed Qilin into a clearing. Although they walked in absolute silence, Qilin turned around.

"I knew you were there. This is your last chance to turn back. Are you ready?" She widened her stance and stood confidently in front of them. Phoebe stepped back so that Apollo could do what he came for.

Grabbing a dagger out of the bag, Apollo nodded. "I am ready if you are." As soon as he finished the sentence, Qilin became a blazing ball of fire. Flames radiated from her arms and curled into balls within her hands. Throwing the fire at Apollo, she moved forward. Apollo ducked the flames and tried to get into an offensive position.

Ace whined next to Phoebe. Leaning down, she patted his head reassuringly. In reality, she was shaking in fear. Still unused to the world of daemons, the fiery daemon before her was a frightening surprise. She felt less terrible about the possibility of Qilin's death. The daemon before her was far from defenseless. Before this moment, how many other potential leaders had tried to kill Qilin and failed?

Qilin threw another ball of fire and it singed Apollo's heels. The grass in the clearing was quickly becoming torched by their fight. Ball after ball of fire was thrown and Apollo managed to shrug it off without any difficulties. Unfortunately, he was unable to stand long enough to get close to her. It was too late when he realized that he should have just used a gun. Rolling away from another ball of fire, he quickly darted in the opposite direction. The sudden change of direction surprised Qilin, and she let the ball of fire go too soon. It released from her hand and flew directly toward Phoebe. Apollo either did not notice where the fire was headed or did not care. He adjusted his stance and lifted the dagger behind his head to throw it.

If you enjoyed this sample then look for **The Shifter - The Daemon Paranormal Romance Chronicles, Book 2**.

Here is a preview of **another story** you may enjoy:

Heart Surrendered: Obsessed Bounty Hunter Romance Series - Book 2 by Carla Coxwell

JACQUI CHUGGED the water from the container like a thirsty beast. She just couldn't get enough of it. Water never tasted so good, better than an orgasm, Jacqui thought, as she splashed some straight into her face. Jacqui was parched, grimy, and her body ached like she just came through a meat grinder. She was up at 0400 hours in her jogging suit and trainers. Uncle Max met her at the door of a building that resembled a huge hangar.

When Uncle Max said yesterday that training started today before the crack of dawn, Jacqui thought he meant some light exercises that would involve some sit-ups and jumping jacks. She was never further from the truth. The next couple of hours had been the most intensive Jacqui ever subjected her body to. And she knew this was just the start.

Uncle Max led her through a routine of squats and crunches, lunges and hamstring curls until her ass had no more feeling left in them. "C'mon Jacqui, move that body," Uncle Max shouted like a drill sergeant. Then he moved on to pull ups, sit-ups, bicep curls, and bench press. Her arms and legs felt disconnected from her body. Her hand was shaking so hard she almost dropped the water bottle she was holding. She was grateful for the fifteen minute break the old man gave her.

"Alright, Jacqui… back to work…" Uncle Max shouted from the sidelines.

She wanted to complain but didn't have the courage to. When she arrived yesterday, Uncle Max told her exactly what to expect for the next couple of weeks. He was dead serious as he went through the program with her. If he was trying to discourage her, he almost succeeded. But Jacqui was too proud to say it. She had come this far to become a bounty hunter.

Before she even got settled into the bedroom that would be hers during her stay, Uncle Max talked to her privately in what he called his 'interrogation room.' It was a small building at the back of the property. The walls were lined with an assortment of maps indicating the different states of the United States. There were yellow pins tacked on certain cities within the map. Jacqui looked around curiously. She noticed the different surveillance gadgets like GPS tracking, high resolution cameras, night vision goggles, an assortment of pens, and spy gear which she was seeing for the first time in her life.

A bank of television sets was stacked near the wall manned by a single individual. Jacqui saw it was streaming live from some part of the country she did not recognize. A huge glass cabinet held an assortment of guns, some she recognized from her dad's own collection.

"Take a seat Jacqui," Uncle Max indicated a wooden table with hardback chairs in a small corner of the room. He did not speak for some time and Jacqui had a strong desire to squirm under his intense gaze.

"Are you sure this is what you want because right now I am here to tell you, it's not going to be an easy life," Uncle Max said. Jacqui nodded her head, indicating she understood. When she came to her decision back home on the night she called Uncle Max, she quit her job the very next day. She told her boss she wanted to do some travelling. Her boss gave her the go-signal. "It's probably what you need right now," he even said.

Jacqui wasn't sure what Uncle Max thought about the whole idea. She hadn't heard from him since she made the call. But a few days later she found an envelope that was left on her porch. There was no forwarding address and it didn't look like it came by mail. Inside was a one-way ticket to Utah and strict instructions what to bring along. Only a small backpack was needed for the clothing list. It became pretty obvious this was not going to be some luxurious holiday.

She was met at the airport by a burly, bald-headed man, wearing dark sunglasses on a stern face. He reminded Jacqui of an ex-marine or military man. He ushered her into a waiting SUV, got behind the wheel, and started the engine.

They left the city behind until all Jacqui could see were tall mountain ranges in the distance. A few miles onward, they turned into a small dirt road and followed a winding path until Jacqui noticed a copse of large evergreen trees where they seemed to be headed. The trees covered a large expanse of land, save for small clearings with structures that resembled warehouses or large barns. They drove past these until they came to a smaller building where she saw Uncle Max waiting by the door. He greeted her warmly, but Jacqui sensed a certain formality in his demeanor.

Looking at him now, sitting behind the table with a grim expression on his face, Jacqui was suddenly filled with an overwhelming insecurity. Did she make the right decision after all? But Jacqui remembered the downward spiral she was on. The sex with random guys. The orgasms she needed to get some sleep so she could stop thinking about the tragic events of her life. And she needed a purpose… to find some meaning in her life. To honor her dad's memory so she would never forget. For her mom who supported him all the way, and for Danny, who was never given the chance to experience what life was all about.

"Yes, Uncle Max. I have never been surer about anything in my life," she declared with a certain degree of conviction. Uncle Max smiled, and for the first time since she arrived, Jacqui felt relieved. She knew whatever lay ahead, Uncle Max wouldn't spare her, wouldn't try to make things easy for her. She knew that.

"Ok then, let's get you started. I am The Agency. I will be responsible for your training. You will not question my decisions… you will do as I say. The training will be rigorous because you will meet all kinds of low-life scumbags. A lot of times your life will be in danger. But you will be trained in self-defense and handling weapons until I feel that you are totally capable of protecting yourself out there. Then and only then will I send you out on a mission. Is that clear?"

Uncle Max asked. Jacqui nodded her head in agreement.

"Alright, settle in. You will be shown to your room. Tomorrow your training starts. And for the next couple of days you will only remember pain," The old man warned her. He wasn't kidding. After five hours of the most intense exercise routines she had ever done, Jacqui couldn't even remember her name. Her body hurt even in places she didn't know existed. And this was just her first day in boot camp.

Lunch had been sparse, with just some fish and vegetables. She was given an hour to rest inside her room which was composed of a bunk bed and a footlocker for her personal stuff. No TV, no telephone, no computer or laptop. Then she was called back again and told to run around a circuit she didn't even notice earlier in the day. She tried counting in her head the number of times she completed a circuit before fatigue settled in and lost count completely. It took all her will power to put one leg in front of the other. By the time Uncle Max called for a halt, dusk had settled and stars appeared brightly in a cloudless sky.

"Supper will be brought to your room. Tomorrow we do the whole routine again," Uncle Max declared before he left. It wasn't a request. It was an order. Jacqui trudged slowly back to her room. There is no time to dwell on the unfamiliarity and sparse surroundings. The bed was a most welcome sight and calling her name. She groaned in pain as she stretched her arms over her head to remove her workout clothes.

Her back was racked with pain as she bent to unlace her trainers.

Jacqui managed to splash some water onto her face before falling face down into the soft covers with only her undies on. Sleep came easy for Jacqui that night. A sleep so deep she hardly noticed the appearance of two figures in her room.

"You think she'll make it?" an older voice inquired. "I don't know Uncle Max. You put her through the wringer today," the other replied. Uncle Max sighed as he looked at the sleeping form of the girl on the bed. "You're hoping maybe she'll give up and just go back home?" the second figure asked curiously.

"Yes… this kind of life isn't for her. She's been through a lot already. But I also can't accept throwing her life away with all those men in strange hotel rooms," Uncle Max replied. "Well… you said the same thing about me too, remember? I didn't turn out too badly," the younger man said. "No, Adam, you are doing very well. The fact is… you will play an important role in this girl's future," Uncle Max replied.

"I can hardly wait…" Adam replied, taking in the full breasts and rounded ass of the sleeping form on the bed. "Just learn to keep that cock of yours inside your pants…" warned the old man, with a hint of indulgence in his voice.

The two figures departed slowly out of the room where Jacqui Schneider slept an exhausted, dreamless sleep.

If you enjoyed this preview then look for **Heart Surrendered: Obsessed Bounty Hunter Romance Series - Book 2 by Carla Coxwell**.

Other Books by Darla Dunbar

- The Romeo Alpha BBW Paranormal Shifter Romance Series

- Romeo Alpha Blood Lines Romance Series

- The Alpha Feud BBW Paranormal Shifter Romance Series

- The Alpha Packed BBW Paranormal Shifter Romance Series

- The Daemon Paranormal Romance Chronicles

- The Mind Talker Paranormal Romance Series

Get the latest update on new releases from the author at:

https://darladunbar.com/newsletter/

About the Author - Darla Dunbar

Darla has been interested in paranormal romance since she was a teenager in high school. It was then that she discovered she could fulfill her fantasies through her writing.

Observing people and human behavior in the area of romance has always been one of her favorite pastimes. Combining that with an overactive imagination is a sure fire way of coming up with interesting themes.

Connect with Darla Dunbar

I really appreciate you reading my book! Here are my social media coordinates:

Friend me on Facebook: https://www.facebook.com/darladunbar/

Follow me on Twitter: https://twitter.com/DarlDunbar

Check me out on Goodreads: https://www.goodreads.com/author/show/8425857.Darla_Dunbar

Subscribe to my newsletter: https://darladunbar.com/newsletter/

Visit my website: https://darladunbar.com/